# Ending with Music

# Maurice Mierau

# Ending with Music

Brick Books

National Library of Canada Cataloguing in Publication Data

Mierau, Maurice, 1962-
  Ending with music

Poems.
ISBN 1-894078-23-3

I. Title.

PS8576.I2858E52 2002    C811'.54    C2002-902873-6
PR9199.3.M45483E52 2002

We gratefully acknowledge the Canada Council for the Arts, the Government of Canada through the Book Publishing Industry Development Program (BPIDP), and the Ontario Arts Council for their support of our publishing program.

The cover photo of the Washington Avenue Bridge in Minneapolis is by Daniel Corrigan. The American poet John Berryman ended his life by jumping off this bridge on January 7, 1972.

The author photograph was taken by Jeremy Clemens-Mierau.

The book is set in Meta and Minion.

Design and layout by Alan Siu

Printed and bound by Sunville Printco Inc.

Brick Books
431 Boler Road, Box 20081
London, Ontario   N6K 4G6

brick.books@sympatico.ca

*to my mother, the story teller*

There are facts in these poems and stories. Some of them have never been written down before. Some are true.

# Table of Contents

## Family and Others

## Murders

**Ending with music**

# Family and Others

do you understand this?  where we came from?
it all adds up
figure it out for yourself

    – Patrick Friesen, *The Shunning*

# My mother at 25

She looks straight at the camera, the wind barely lifts her dress
in the 50s the white clapboard church in the background
signifies

no back
sliding
no sermon
with more than three points

no idling
gossip
no books
but the bible
minimum sex, maximum starch.

My aunts' and uncles' faces sharpen, fade out
the sound of the four part hymn washes them
faces blistered in music,
tenor and bass dance slippery
with her mother's husky alto,

her father recites poems about shipwrecked sailors
saved by God's hand on oceans
none of them have ever seen, they are land-locked in
the middle of a five year drought.

*Beneath the cross of Jesus I fain would take my stand,*
*The shadow of a mighty rock Within a weary land*

*A home within the wilderness, A rest upon the way,*
*From the burning of the noontide heat, And the burden of the day*

They are all in tears, except my mother
at 25 she looks straight at whoever's

holding the camera, her dress lifts
with the wind, barely, she sees me.

# Norman Vincent Peale visits Saskatchewan, 1933

The words of the Bible are powerful THOUGHT CONDITIONERS.

–Norman Vincent Peale

Our cousins were running
for real estate jobs, away from the cranks,
heading west, sunning
themselves in bottle blondes,
churches with endless parking lots, commercial cunning

"Since happiness and effectiveness depend upon the kind of
thoughts we think, it is absolutely impossible to be happy if we
think unhappiness-producing thoughts."

Peter Schultz the grocer had a doublebreasted suit
but wore patched clothes for the relief line,
Grandpa got migraines when his shift
started at the railroad, splitting pine
logs for ties, wrecking his back, he lay there moaning.
Grandma said it was a bad headache,
so bad he didn't get up for three months

"This text will help you avoid a nervous breakdown. It will
stimulate your recovery if you have had one."

A dog pissed around his territory, scrappier
than us by a long shot –
this was the year we sold the Model T for food – happier
than standing in line in the hot

summer, this was the year nothing was fair,
Schultz tore down the fence,
letting his cattle graze our fields bare
and Grandpa said nothing about rents

He stayed on his land
while the dust made ravines around his mouth
his face dry and cracked and
he never thought west or south

## Memento

*Version 1, hymn*

She remembers his recitations
at tent-meetings, his voice
with a cry like Jimmy the Blue Yodeller,
his letting the chores go for weeks
to practice the break
in his voice at the climax –

*Then they listened. He is singing*
*"Jesus, Lover of my soul!"*

The tent lifts off the ground, again
his pure tenor echoes like a steel guitar, remember
a stone in an azure pool, hair
in a locket his face glows at the wedding feast

*Then the watchers, looking homeward*
*Through their eyes with tears made dim,*
*Said, "He passed to be with Jesus*
*In the singing of that hymn."*

And when he stopped again
it was like there was no memory
of rain even, but a stream of wet hair
on his face,

She remembers she stopped
praying for it then, everyone
stopped praying, the tent floated gently
and after the service

he pins the brooch over her breast, again
she never forgets or remembers quite
how
gently

## Version 2, Alzheimer's

In the nursing home my grandmother is 18 again,
she smells the sweet alfalfa on his hair,
the smoke on his breath: she remembers
the night of the wedding, she is wearing
Depends and the staff don't always
stop her from walking out on the road.

*The smoke makes a stairway for you to descend,*
*You come to my arms may this bliss never end*

> This is not a story I really believe.
> I made up the smoke on his breath
> to link it with the song lyric. My grandfather never
> smoked. I don't know how alfalfa smells.

A preacher came to the home on Sunday; again
he said remember
to pray, his hair
a mantle of light snow, a wedding
gown.

> This is a story I tell to replace
> theirs, the one they never wrote.
> It's a true story, but not about them.

My grandmother cannot remember the act of prayer.
She sees the silver brooch, remembers
he gave it, with a locket of their first child's hair,
she remembers pinning it on her best Sunday dress,
carefully, like a song lyric on a strange new melody.

*Awake or asleep every memory I'll keep*
*deep in a dream of you.*

*Version 3, Grandma's diary*

What happens when the story you tell
yourself stops making sense?

At the end of Grandma's life when the children
came to town, Grandpa pretended
that she cooked the meals. (There were subtle differences
my mother knew later, the amount of dill
in the borscht, the extra sugar in everything.)

He was strong
again, he told stories about the weather
(why was Grandma's diary always about
the weather?) and the crops
and church, and they hung together.

June 4
Had a nice sprinkle at night — but not a real rain,
it's cloudy & dreary also cool, seemingly we have
lots of cloudy days but not decent rain, for which
we so very much wait.

The doctor said it was nerves again
as she remembers
the depression maybe
she soils herself on the way out of the nursing home,

she sees him half a life ago
shuddering on the bed
gasping like something just born
and then not moving for a week
and after, silence.

Then, falling, onto the newly laid asphalt
outside the nursing home, the smell of rain,
she forgets the names of her children.

June 4
Got a white set of gloves & scarf, flower hat, a
purse, & a pair of black flatties 5.99.

... Hung out everything today, it's windy but bright
& sunny, & no dust.

she falls onto the wet asphalt
the smell of rain where

2 years earlier he pulled the blanket over her
for a Sunday nap, adds some dill
to the soup, goes
to his own room, humming
a sad hymn, trying
to see how it ends.

# Grandfather, retired, dreams a tell-tale heart

He sits in a wheelchair beside me looking
at Lake Diefenbaker, to him the waters
of the Saskatchewan are the flowering
of the desert, the baptism of irrigation
pleases him.

*But sleep won't come*
*the whole night through*

A loudspeaker carries the church service into his room
in the home, but he turns it off most Sundays
> and hums Wilf Carter and Hank Williams tunes
> to himself.

June 1962
It was a horrible day, oh, so hot and dry, in the
evening at 7 o'clock we had a terrible dust
storm, it sure looked awful, and also some rain
but not enough to make the potatoes grow.

He would like to be on his son's combine.
> Grandpa covered his yard in concrete
> because it was
> less than a section of land, useless.

*When tears come down like falling rain*
*you'll toss around and call my name*

Look at these fields he says:
this is what paradise will be like.

## What Uncle Tiny said about women
*for Betsy*

If you walk into the door without reaching
for the knob you're in love.

If you can't remember her name when you look
at her father's nose you're in love.

If you smell her stronger than beef steak or blood
strong and you know it's her you're in love

If you open a window by putting your hand
through glass you're in love

When you can't feel the warm blood on your hands
her thighs

If you want her hands, her mouth, her ass, her name
when you want a window
when you want a wall
(when you want her)

you're in love

# Easter morning, Jamaica, 1973

In the beginning is
the feeling that drives
you home at night
that makes you see

the furrow where the stone was rolled away
oh holy day that raised
this force through green

wet tropical sun-dappled rain
replenishes day every time in this
season and drops in the dust –
smeared every day

the splendid world is crushed
and raised up on the seventh or
at least annually the preacher's huge
voice recalls that first break

the clearing where God spoke
and you couldn't tell anyone
until you didn't believe anymore
and you revised the story as a joke

but now still in the moment
your heart sponging like a perfect
catastrophe, full with the next stroke,
systole, diastole, flow-through

You can't hear what the preacher says
and after will never remember
just the conviction, heart-sense
something you usually don't know.

## Buffalo Plains Hospital

My grandfather is dying in Buffalo Plains Hospital:
the white light over his bed shows
the skin shrivelling on his face
and on the bright yellow sheet
the stub of his right ring finger gleams –

a 1945 Ford tractor fan belt chewed it off.
Grandpa was a conscientious objector; the missing
joint was his sacrifice to the war effort.

Politics is just like war, he said – all lies,
all made up. There's truth in nature and
the Bible, mostly the New Testament,
nobody made that up
in the dust from the summer fallow
in the muck at the bottom of a coulee
after a summer rain.

# Hundreds of seagulls

**1.**

On his deathbed my grandfather soon finds
that he's tired of waiting, too sick to get up.
In our minds we see him pace the room,
glancing at his newly hairless wrist, the plastic cup.

**2.**

That day a white seagull
lands on the hospital roof.

Maybe the bird is prairie-born, dull
with rooting in garbage, but a bit aloof.

(My uncle remembers a symbolic tableau of geese
in the sky, not these noisy gulls.)

There are hundreds of kinds of seagulls
native to the prairies, this is not a fiction.

**3.**

Are you close to the Lord?
He asked me in Kansas, near the end
of the Vietnam war, when nearness to
some idea of God still mattered,

his ideas all in the flat breasts
of the rented wheat field
where he worked out tests
of the Lord's presence that yielded

nothing.

**4.**

My grandfather died right after the ten o'clock news
looking at his hairless wrist, maybe for the time
though no one knows,
seagulls flying off the roof
as if it were their last day in Saigon.

No one knows where they flew.

## Uncle Tiny speculates on theological limits

Hollywood lives in the pink sequins on the preacher's stetson,
radio carries him and his chap-slapping rope

through vacuum tubes, formica, wood and ether
all over the flat wintry countryside.

In darkest Africa they have no radios
the unsaved are going to hell by the thousands per minute

my uncle Tiny wonders why they go to hell
if they have no radios.

He is outside watching the north light
up on the Tabernacle's cowboy preacher night,

his soul is oozing onto his mother
of pearl belt inlays like a blood stain,

he remembers that Gene Autry
is also going to hell and smiles with disdain.

## Nancy (or I was Frank Sinatra)

The only photo you
ever gave me you weren't smiling, it was monochrome

you weren't laughing either I knew right away that you
would end up teaching in a girl's school

that you were on the rebound that
you rejected a guy with a six-figure career

or a dreadful Manchurian candidate complex, depending
how his cards fell

Everything about you was controlled except
when I held you that one time and touched your

small perfect breasts shouting we could
stay up forever your hands on my butt

I met you in a Mexican restaurant in Victoria, drunk
and picturesque, without my hat, take me back, take me back

I wrote you when I had my first girl, said it was you

We watched Italian movies that summer, *La Dolce Vita*,
Mastroianni coolly surrounded by black spaghetti bra straps

I was lost in your form-fit turtleneck, holding your
European tour and knowing your brief need of me

Hold me again. Hold me again. Nobody gets the medal
of honour in this one

## What I really want

What I want is to be like Rilke
proudly display my scars from carrying the name
Maria, wear dresses,
go to military academy,
write letters to young poets

Hang out in large gloomy castles
with beautiful rich women who
make me tea and don't
go to bed with me

Suffer horrendously for my
art in the most picturesque
Italian settings while never
having a day job what

I really want is to see
the angels he saw
to believe that I could
change everything
with words

## After that, teenagers

pushing past the entrance
falling out of muscle cars
squeezing through rings of jacketed
kids, sure that this day mattered

more than anything I
matter each said except
a few sadder ones who already
knew better but fell

out of the muscle cars
running looking normal yelling
(being kids they thought like grownups)
they were tight and sober

sunlight dispersed over them
washed slowly past their
speeding heads none of them knew
that they moved in a different way
after that

## Escape

fumbling in the dashboard light, finding
the dreamed-for bra strap,
hiding cigarettes and understanding baseball
metaphors already like the great code
of some knowable literature – not the strange country of

marriage, mortgages, missed menstrual cycles excluding
Alpine heights, unconquered books, victories
abandoned at dawn, romantic unquenchable loneliness,
French cigarettes with synesthesiac names, adolescent escape

from this small town with its fat thighs
clamped tightly around my ears pounds with
Mr. Eliot's coffee spoons rattling, surrounds me
like some new sound technology, filling
an empty golden bowl

## Musicians in love

*for Tony M.*

I fell asleep in your room, she walked out when she saw me
no rose in my teeth, just a little spit dribbling from one corner

of my mouth, thank god nobody talked just
then although there was a chorus we could have repeated

over and over, your hand on her, me lying on the floor,
insensible, you watching her walk out, flesh shaking.

Trouble is your business, her kind of trouble is
you, she has a black heart, she has hair

down to her ass, right down to where your hand runs
up her thigh, trying to find a vein wanting

to push the needle in or out, falling in
deeper until all you smell is what your hand found

but never her, she kept pushing you and you
could have had anyone she said but never.

Sometimes you phone me in the
middle of the night like Glenn Gould, I remind you

that she had a dark moustache, looked like the Great
Dictator but with a big ass, you don't care it's love

even these conversations in your head are wordless
you wake up at night repeating her name and shouting

there is more to it than just sex you said, but isn't
that always the way, you wanted somebody to watch over

you wanted somebody, not her. You feel your hands
on her leg pushing up the skirt so slowly

that duration stops seeming like a French word she's given
up everything before you

tell her most of what we say
is just words, words are getting in the way,

she can't believe what you won't say.

## Watching Wim Wenders with Mike

In this shot
there are a million grey shades

The road is receding behind the camera
there is a desolation in the passing electrical lines

that looks the same in Germany, Texas,
or the prairies, the women

are untouchable, they know everything
the only writers are children

the pornography is beautiful
the faces interesting, a loon

is either crazy or a bird
every movie ends

with someone tearing something up
or just driving off alone

## Silent referendum

I am tired of setting record cold snaps
I am tired of the weather
I am tired of the news and the sun.

None of it prevents tracking you down
and writing this,
I swore that nothing would.

When will you explain what you did?

Now I am tired of driving to work
with news on the radio
the clock on the dashboard, Timex
on my wrist, clock on my virtual desktop panel,
the time beside the caller ID on my phone.

When will you explain what you did?
The traffic continues to crawl, forward.

I am tired of waiting for things to change
for the gods to be propitious, software to uninstall
for the clocks to run backwards while toilets unflush.
I am tired of money and its accumulation,
I am tired of waiting
for inspiration to descend from the badly dyed curtains.

When will you explain what you did?
I don't see how it could affect the weather or the dollar.

I am tired of waiting for the ethnic vote
in my head to swing around
and say something universally intelligible.

I am tired of waiting
for you to explain.

# The vision thing

The day Aunt Mary died
I was busy consoling myself.

(My son is not HIV positive,
My marriage is better than Tolstoy's.

My income is within the national average,
I voted for the government.)

Aunt Mary was simple-minded
because of childhood meningitis she

was heroic and cheerful. Aunt Mary's vision stopped
her from dying, she saw her parents at the end of her bed

calling from over the river, Mary come be with the dead
but she said no, there is still work for me to do

in the seniors' home, folding fresh laundry
singing hymns, cheering invalids.

When Mary finally gave in and died
the funeral home director had a flowered tie.

He talked smoothly about death,
his teeth were white with sincerity.

During the service we sang "How Great Thou Art" in four part harmony.
It was better than a Billy Graham show.

I knew Mary expected to sing with the angels,
she could see them at the foot of her bed.

She could see all of us from over there.
She could see us eating dainties at her funeral.

I drove back to work squinting at the sun. Why can't I see properly?
Why do the angels have to sing in tune?

## *Casablanca* at 40 below

You loved me but were married
to some dream of the past or future.

Everything you said to me was true
except from my limited, wise-cracking perspective.

Nothing I said was true, and
I was from a nation of drunkards who don't feel anything.

What was really scary was when I
started doing the thinking for both of us.

Then in my weakness, I allowed duelling national anthems
and began drinking with customers.

So I put you on the plane
with your movies and started work on the next deal.

A beautiful relationship begun with someone
whose heart was his least vulnerable part,

or were you just rounding up ghosts,
the usual suspects?

# Church going

*for Harry L.*

Sundays it can always be found here
in a place without incense or fertility rites,
harmony singing, four-wheel drives,

the churchgoers where I attend
want their bodies healed, kids safe,
the massage parlours and booze cans closed,
the word of the Lord, monogamous signifier
married in the blood of the signified.

Jesus cleared the temple of moneylenders
and writers his life rooted in
speech acts, the perfect word
in a world beyond perverse versions.

I respect their infinite twelve step program
that clutches and pushes toward an unceremonious god,
no respecter of twelve steps
or tones.

Sundays, beneath it all, desire runs
like a steeplechase runner for water,
like a tenor for breath
like these people, wanting something I can't name,
and beneath it all, still going.

## He was calm but elated

*for Randall Jarrell*

He was barefoot that night and the gravel
on the hospital road pushed against his feet,
it was not like wearing a tennis shoe,
the clay court solid like an
extension of your legs.

Or maybe he was wearing shoes,
black leather shoes. He could feel almost
none of the space between his toes
that tennis shoes give you.

He veered into the road thinking
about the gash on his wrist
but not trying to.
He was not trying to move quickly
when the car hit him.

Or he veered into the road
deliberate, conscious, finishing
the job he started with a razor,
a perfect clarity in his movements
like an overhand kill mid-court.

Or he never veered into the road at all –
the car chased him at the edge
driven by a Manchurian candidate
throwing him into the trees and back
amazingly light and terribly damaged.

# Murders

# Why this version is unbelievable

What we don't say is
how my father watched,
while his mother pushed all those men
into lost envelopes, before she died
when he was ten.

What we want to believe is something else
(What we don't say is).
My grandmother saw
whole families come
to the river and walk
in till the water rose

over their heads. Other families ran
into barns. They poured kerosene
(What we want to believe is something else)
over themselves. (Do you believe
that? She also said the KGB was
run by the Jewish banking conspiracy.)

What we let ourselves believe is different than
this version. My grandmother
(do you believe this?) was the regimental whore, she did what
she had to. Whisky
started to taste good. There's always some guy on PBS saying

depression is a form of illness, suicide is caused by untreated depression.
But people do anything to live until a dead
calm replaces the smell of soiled underwear like
a logical state. (What we want to believe is
something else.)

There were many things we didn't
say when the war was over
the only thing was getting to

a new world, surviving,
Prozac, high speed Internet.

What we don't say is
why we want to believe
what we won't let ourselves
believe.

## Soldiers

They marched wobbling into our yard, drunk
as the fish in the pool. They threw grenades

into the water, lily-pads exploding in soft white pieces,
frog heads jumping on the grass.

That afternoon they lay on top of our neighbour's wife
while she screamed more and more quietly.

## Amish wedding hymn

The martyr Hans Haslibach will not recant.
At his death three signs will prove his innocence:

>*As his head is severed from his body it leaps into his hat*
>
>*The sun turns red*
>
>*The town pump flows blood*

The martyr Hans Haslibach will not recant
as you now sing for 32 stanzas
standing up in wooden churches on hard pews
at weddings.

# Uncle Joe's couch

Never marry till you can say to yourself that you have done all you are capable of doing, and till you have ceased loving the woman you have chosen and can see her clearly, or you will make a cruel and irrevocable mistake.

– Prince Andrei Bolkonsky in *War and Peace*

He began by throwing the couch through the window. His mistress left him because he wasn't cultured enough, even though he wrote poems filled with burning cigarettes, and he wrote them in bed, just the way Nina Simone warned against. What is culture anyway, my mother said.

When Uncle Joe's couch with the checkerboard pattern flew through his picture window, the neighbour telephoned my mother and she told my father at dinner. My mother said Uncle Joe's French mistress has left him because of his drinking and so he's thrown that big green couch through the window.

I could see Uncle Joe heaving the couch, shards of window glass flying, frozen like a snapshot in the air.

When Uncle Joe got drunk the next day and shot the neighbour's cat with his son's BB gun, the neighbour called again. At dinner my mother said Uncle Joe's unhappy because back in Russia the girl he loved wouldn't marry him and so he married her sister out of spite. She left him twenty years later.

Uncle Joe's French mistress kissed me on the cheek once, she smelled like garlic and sweet flowers, her lips were very red.

When Uncle Joe chopped up his couch with an axe and burned it on the lawn, there was a picture in the *Winnipeg Tribune*. My mother said Uncle Joe is a sad man who let women and drink ruin his life.

In the picture it looks like Uncle Joe is standing in the fire, there is smoke coming out of his head and he's waving the axe.

# What you can't write about

War is an event ... counter to human reason and human nature.

– Tolstoy, *War and Peace*

When you find out you can kill someone
then you know what you can't write about.

Killing someone is more personal
than having sex with them
(although it's standard military practice
to combine the two).

When you know what it's like to want revenge
more than life itself
and when you get it
(there's nothing new to say about this)
you still hate stronger than
anything,
stronger than you wanted any woman.

When you see thousands of dead bodies
on a field
(I know literature is a lousy witness)
soldiers taking turns on a young girl
or any of the things
that make people say yes
that's war, as if it were like the weather,
uncontrollable but strangely part of us.

# Looking for words, repeating them

> Napoleon was drawn into Russia, not as the result of any plan (no one ever
> believed in such a possibility), but simply through a complex interplay
> of intrigues, aims, and wishes .… Everything happened fortuitously.
>
> — Tolstoy, *War and Peace*

Turning over the fresh corpses of Russian soldiers
he reached into pockets and bags
for documents.

Uncle Joe stripped dead bodies
of letters to sweethearts, mothers, etc.,
often the blood made pages stick
together so they were
hard to read. But he read them
all for the Germans.

In the two years he spent searching
dead letters
for military intelligence he found
nothing but tenderness, foolish rhetoric
and anger.

Many of the soldiers wrote letters like
politicians write speeches, one for
winning, one for losing, one for
living, one for not.

Joe sees her begging on her knees
her breasts pushing up like burial mounds
on a rapidly filled trench.
He explains that she will die
for reporting German tank movements
to the Russians. He repeats
words from another language. Her
beauty is palpable, there is no time, she thinks
it will save her. It won't. He repeats
the words.

## Breakfast at the concentration camp

Standing in columns with the other prisoners
in uniforms that look like comic pajamas,
burning your insides
with boiling hot soup
mostly water (bad) with bits of cabbage
you have to burn your insides
because after 30 seconds exactly
(almost) they start shooting from
the tower,
burning
holes in your guts

# The brotherhood
*for my father*

The institution continues to be dominated by a graveyard across the street.

The board wants to shield students from confusion. Truth is a narrow bed, easily measured. The history professor says dizziness leads to balance, that an excessive grip on the present is just a form of spiritual Alzheimer's.

Afterwards no one knows who started shouting or when the professor turned burn-red in the face, what kind of an accident made him drop like a rock. Massive coronary.

Afterwards no one tells the widow what was discussed in the meeting. Words are neutral communication vehicles, like police cars, harmless in themselves. No one ever tells the widow. This is a brotherhood. They have rules.

The institution continues to be dominated by a graveyard across the street. Afterwards the dead are unhappy too, the city can't afford to cut the grass.

My father is on a subway in Toronto when he hears about his friend, the dead professor. He turns white. Surrounded by Nigerian university students he looks preposterously white.

He will be sick for three days. Not even the Blue Jays winning the pennant race will console him.

## Leonhard Keyser, who would not burn

The priests spoke Latin to Leonhard Keyser
as he was wheeled in the cart to the fire
but he answered them in German
so the people could understand.

Then Leonhard Keyser leaned down from the cart,
plucked a flower with his tied hands, and said to the judge:
> Lord judge, here I pluck a flower;
> if you cannot burn both this flower and me
> then you must consider what you have done
> and repent.

And therefore when the wood was entirely consumed
his body was taken from the fire uninjured,
rolling out on the opposite side with
the unwithered flower in his hand,
his skin still smooth and white.

Then the three executioners cut him alive into pieces
which they cast into the fire, but they
succeeded only in burning the wood.

## Srebrenica

Beauty is always elsewhere
dipping her lovely toe in the water
that's too hot
or not warm enough

She puckers her wide beautifully adapted mouth
(a vagina dentata in case you were wondering)
at you and barely
as the water rises to her valentine-
shaped ass and shots are fired at you in the dream

a red sports car leads you
to the stadium, scarred asphalt
parking lots, a crowded stinking bus

Alsatian dogs and 9" knives gripped in swollen
hands, beauty is elsewhere as
neighbours beckon you
off the truck and beat you
senselessly, remorselessly

## Tall George Wagner

Tall George Wagner did not believe
that water baptism had saving power
or that the priest forgave your sins
or leavened bread with words.

Tall George Wagner was tormented
and the prince's tutor
and George Wagner's wife and child
all urged him to recant.

(Why didn't he? He could have
just relaxed or gone shopping.
Other than contributing this folk tale
to the *Martyrs' Mirror*, what good
did he do? Why the hell was he so happy?)

Because George Wagner was immovable
the executioner took him
to the middle of the city.
There a bag of powder was tied to his neck
his face did not pale
nor his eyes show fear.
He happily offered his spirit up
on the eighth day of February, 1527.

# Revenge stories

## 1 The Bridge

Since he refused to die in his lord's private army
his lord's priests took him
to the bridge outside town.

(This was where he had the first
vision, when the devil stepped out
of his space ship and gave him the weapon.)

They tied his hands and dumped
him in the river. He said
"no one shall pass over this bridge again!"

(In the second vision he learned
how to touch the exploding switch
in his mind that activated the bomb.)

That evening a violent
flood washed away
the bridge.

(Then others had the vision, a bridge
to another world.)

## 2  Nose for a Head

when the executioner struck off the man's head something flew
off his face so he put up his hands

(no one saw what it was or why he put his hands up but some
said they saw a black hen he tried whisking away and

others said it was a demon with shears
dancing and glinting in the sun) but everybody soon saw

the executioner's nose drop off which was
definitely God.

## 3  Gospel Song

Tempted and tried, we're oft made to wonder
why it should be thus all the day long,
while there are others
living about us, never molested though in the wrong.

– "Farther Along"

In AD 1529 George Bauman was arrested
in Banschlet, for his faith and his eagerness to die.

After application of the rack, assorted torture and a lie
Bauman recanted twice in church.

On his way to church for the third time
he had a vision of a peacock with 500 feathers

beckoning to him, untying the priest's tethers
calling from the gates of heaven.

So Bauman did not recant, but confessed
his faith, defied the priests and revoked

their creed, while the extorters choked
on their elegant gruel.

He sang on his way to the death place,
happy, and when his shoes stuck in the village mud

he sang like the last bird left after the flood,
he kicked off his shoes and ran for courage, for joy.

Then he was beheaded with a heavy sword
and the nobleman and all the priests who judged him

came to ends just as grim
dying miserably and in pain as Jesu Christ is our Lord Amen.

# Deformation after Luther

> God is in that city; she will not be overthrown ...
>
> – Psalm 46:5

## 1 Eating the Angel

In Münster we eat horses, roast cats on spears,
fry mice in pans. The grain is gone. The cows
are gone. We send our words in books like fears
surrounding towns and villages. We make no bows

to kings, the sky disappears like a scroll
rolling up. I eat the scroll.
It is sweet but turns sour in my spleen.
A woman gives birth to a dragon, and between
bursts of fire an angel eats the dragon.

The mercenary says that war is cold.
We made war on the heretics. Their old
women would cook for us. One stabbed
our captain with a cooking knife, his eyes crabbed
shut, his blood spraying. We told

the old woman we see the sky disappear
in war time you eat scrolls,
it tastes like sweetmeat you jeer
a woman giving birth to dragons in bowls.

Our mercenaries kill papists, slowly
or quickly we pay four guilders a month and
free plundering. No one signs up. If you eat unholy
wafers you don't get paid. A band
of men begins eating the dead,

I see the sky disappear like a scroll
rolling up into coal dust. I eat it,
the taste souring,
a dragon rips his way out of the womb, towering
between bursts of fire an angel eats the dragon's spleen.

## 2 German Tour

Mercenaries climb the walls like ants after sugar
and the townspeople drop boiling lime,
burning pitch-soaked rags and rocks on their heads, still
mercenaries climb the walls like ants after sugar.

They cut captured mercenaries open across the waist, intestines
oozing over steel like the bishop's promises – free plundering
for mercenaries, safe passage for surrendering townspeople,
they cut captured mercenaries open across the waist, intestines
        oozing over steel.

Blood scurries, then pours in red rivulets from her blazing white
        throat,
she is executed by Leyden, God's self-anointed king of the town,
who repossessed her from a greedy elder, no respect for words
        or authority,
blood scurries, then pours in red rivulets from her blazing
        white throat.

They nail paper to Leyden
after the town is on fire. This man is a heretic
with broken legs, they remove his tongue and cage, he tours
        Germany alive and dead,
they nail paper to Leyden.

## The difference between a martyr and a suicide

The sack bursting open off
a high bridge to expel this
man I admire, a martyr –

not an eloquent suicide

(not that he didn't cling to the sack
his fingers an unspeakable confession
playing an inaudible instrument),

the town executioner struck him blind
with a stick: oh how you murder me –

this man like a frog falling heavily
into stagnant water, I pity you,
the sack bursting open –

a martyr who could not live
in the flesh
drowning in it.

## Uncle George and Nietzsche
*for Vic B.*

He woke up drunk and
18 in a cornfield
at the end of the war.

That morning the Russians caught him right
after he puked
on his German uniform.

*He suffered prostrating attacks of weeping, accompanied by*
*trembling and facial grimaces.*

They stuck him in a camp
where he got thinner than Courtney Cox.

The Russians needed a prisoner who talked Russian
and my uncle (who already spoke Russian) pretended
to learn it in two weeks.  That was when they let him
start reading and gave him bread with his gruel.

Then my uncle was on night duty, he had to stay
awake or they'd shoot him.
He read
to stay awake at night, the only books were
*The Three Musketeers* in German
and some Nietzsche. After the adventure
he read Nietzsche.

*Behind the locked door of his room he raved and ranted in a private*
*bacchanal, demented, joyful, naked.*

What my Jesus-loving uncle made
of the eternal recurrence, *amor fati, ecce homo,*
the revaluation of all values, *Twilight of the Idols,*
the tremor of southern light,
I don't know, but he told me this the summer I was 18,
working the night shift at 7-11,

drinking Coke slurpies
and reading Nietzsche to stay awake.

*On January 3, 1889 in the Via Po Nietzsche embraced a cabman's
nag and collapsed on the pavement. He lost his mind then in Turin
and died August 25th, 1900, of a stroke, his face flabby and lifeless,
in his sister's care.*

## My Uncle the SS officer

That place where Mengele performed orderly
experiments on twin children,
that was a different place,
it was not the Russian front where armed adults and
teenagers killed in hot flashes
behind the lines, "God is on our side" on each SS buckle-face.
There was no holiday time off
except
for the occasional
visit to a whore house for health reasons
(like Kafka did after a hard
day at the Austro-Hungarian
workers' compensation board).

My uncle was on the Russian front far away from
the famous Work Will Make You Free places
but nearby were all those ditches dug by the unlucky
dead who lay in them, the unlucky coincidentally
Jewish bodies in a ditch in a little town on the Eastern front

where my uncle's future wife
would pass
two weeks later clutching her Bible
like a tattered bullet-proof vest,
like a charm bracelet of dried garlic cloves,
like a dark blanket,
like a sore.

## Returning to the scene

Fidel & Nikita are negotiating, in 1962, the year after my
    mother stopped bleeding.
I was born during the placement of intermediate range missiles
    in Cuba
while they negotiated on a pier in the Crimea, not speaking
    each other's language,
but speaking to me.

Each image cries out for more bandwidth
as it fills your screen from
alt-binaries.pictures.erotica.pornstar-jenna-jameson
and all the other alt-binaries.

Every paramilitary in the world is thuggish, illiterate
but actually they watch Tom Green on MTV,
read *True Police Cases* magazine, e-mail URLs
on tier-one laptops with large screens.

Eroticism is purely a cover issue
when you wake up with blood on your penis,
(I will come back to this scene)
on your camouflage fatigues, on your field binoculars

(you will come back to this scene too).

It is 1999 and you are negotiating
with yourself over Naugahyde,
meditating on Bond girls still
in the future there is blood
on the steering wheel, on the volume
control, on you.

You read about those Serb rape
camps, that insane guy
shooting his ex-wife with a cross-bow
in Toronto, or the maniac who shot his
wife in front of their kids in a women's
shelter in Hamilton, there is no complicity,
that was a different scene

(you will return to it though, later).

# Ending with music

But suicides have a special language.
Like carpenters they want to know *which tools*.
They never ask *why build*.
>  – Anne Sexton, "Wanting to Die"

Poet, teach us
to love our dying.
>  – Robert Kroetsch, *Seed Catalogue*

## No talking
*for Paul Jr.*

Throw the light away, said the insurance executive
to himself, pulling panty hose over the exhaust pipe.

Things as they were needed to change
on the blue banjo he played in the dark.

How happy he looks at 25, photographed,
young and firmly muscled, immortal.

What do I know about his Fort Garry elegy
what made him retreat in the basement

and finally in the garage. This was what
made us talk at first,

we were both preoccupied
with self-inflicted death, with getting over it,

with consolation.
What made us think we'd console each other?

Turn off the sound, he loved music
but left no voice. No talking

was the rule, his widow said
"let's face it." Let's face the music and dance.

Facing it is the last thing anybody wants,
beauty is running in the mind.

# Night at the opera
*in memory of Mabel Clemens, 1910 – 1995*

84 years old and secretly incontinent,
she avoids liquid all day to go see *Carmen*.

Right at the back of the concert hall, cataracts in place,
she spurns my rented Minolta opera glasses.

So I use them for close-ups of Carmen's barely restrained breasts.
I thought her sight was gone but she reads all the sur-titles.

Carmen's table-dancing rabble-rousing
perfectly pitched appetite suffuses her cheeks

fills her thin protruding veins
with bloody music so

that her legs and arms still hum tunelessly
on the drive home and when she

as always jumps out of the car
it is still moving her life is moving quickly too

*Rigoletto* still looms ahead –
her last season almost over.

# So quietly

*for Carol H., 1962 – 1994*

1

What was it about seeing you that day,
the secret chemical of the past,
the hidden garden gone cancerous
and permanently leached,
a dry cold winter's day, sunny.

I was home sick on the last day before
the chemical solutions kicked in
for you, when all could be well,
joy falling dispensed in well-planned
fragments.

I made you tea and sympathetic noises
when you accused almost everyone we knew
of child abuse, I tried to be objective and
sympathetic, and was failing horribly when
you left for the school, to scream at teachers.

You made the *Winnipeg Sun* the next day,
front page, the ambulance in behind,
tabloid photo balance.  At what point
do you vomit because of what
you do for a living?

2

If it had to be hanging
it should have been more like Ken Saro-Wiwa's
in Nigeria. But this is a winter country,
a quiet place that shrinks pain and the
past so you almost forget.

Your children opened like doors
to the cold air, what
prepared them was your gradual exit,
hospital corridors, absences, appearance,
exit.

Sometimes I think of your air
of violent gentleness, I remember
how lovely, hopeful and young
you looked as your hand trembled
pouring tea.

Before the weekend silence came
with the morning paper, when there was no
pain left to speak,
before the rope
took your breath away, strange
that you died choking, so quietly.

## Suite for Michael

*in memory of Michael Wiebe (1961 – 1985)*

1    The Economy of Feeling

How come death isn't listed on NASDAQ
a high tech corporation whose debt
could be restructured,
why is there
no bull market economy of feeling?

You planned your death carefully and
I tried to keep myself out of this
with language and numbers

but it's always the survivors,
crawling like auditors scrolling through
spreadsheets on infinite screens that
gather dust as they read, staring until eyes shrivel
into myopia, asking hard questions,
figuring out why losses always
end up staggering

## 2   Isn't it romantic

When we were 18 the La Salle Hotel was a romantic place.
Inside it was a scene from Dostoevsky, and I recognized it,
the smell of beer, urine, construction workers, vagrants
(only an 18-year-old could think Dostoevsky romantic).

On the street two drunks embrace.
There are not 13 ways of looking.

But you thought the world of lost fathers
in Paris, Texas was romantic.  You thought
that Wim Wenders movie with the director who gets shot
in monochrome, in LA, a film noir
where nothing happens, you thought that
was romantic.

On the street two drunks embrace.
Even inebriated sentiment can be genuine.

I thought it was romantic that you kept
a journal, wrote down your impressions
of the *Duino Elegies*, Edmonton as a subject
for film, the German New Wave,
Nabokov, meaning
captured like the taste of peppermint in
peppermint Schnapps.

On the street two drunks embrace.
I no longer know what to make
of this.

I thought your death
was beautiful too like Yukio Mishima's
but without the violence, the words
on page after laboured page, or the bad movie,
but your life as a secret project,
a dream
that was beautiful,
unfinished, over.

## 3   In the blue truck

In the blue truck where his uncle found him
there was a mattress for a pillow and
            (cast me not away from your presence)
his flesh had begun to change colour
            (my soul is cast down, it is cast down)

We wanted the blank perfection of memory
at the funeral
we read psalm 51
            (the sacrifices of God are a broken spirit)
there were crocuses on the coffin
I did not look

I wanted the blank perfection of a white page
I wanted to lie down with the corpse
            (my heart is broken now, it is not contrite)

I wanted to live the moment you
started choking in words
instead of the sour smell of gas fumes,
in the blue truck, on the mattress
I wanted to lie down with you
and close my eyes

## 4    Debate

*Gazing up into the darkness you said*
velcro strips hold our brains together,
our genitals are made of silver dollars,
and beauty is nothing in this goddamn strip mall of a culture

*I saw myself as a creature driven and derided by*
the impossibility of goodness,
the way touch lingers only in words,
the falsity of language

vanity you said and showed me your picture of Duino Castle:
write something as good as Rilke and I'll buy you a real castle,

*and my eyes burned with anguish and anger* but at least I was angry

## 5   The end of desire

The end of desire is the last martyrdom, when
the body isn't good enough

> (I have seen a different blankness
> on the faces of pregnant women,
> as if they were rubbed
> with luminous dust)

Not the beginning
but the end,
the last rite –
I chose instead
to be the fly
kicking
in the sticky ointment
of the self

## 6  Dream

I went looking for Michael in heaven
to see if he was there

When I found him
he was making a movie about an angel
who's attacked in the parking lot
of a Burger King but whose
arms aren't long enough to punch back

(it was in depressive German grey scale,
key of D minor)

When I met Michael
he apologized for being there
and told me to go home

# The pain problem

Hear me, O God! / A broken heart, / Is my best part

– Ben Jonson

## 1   Silent movie

The night among concrete
and steel is still with
wet snow falling lightly,
my son and I are walking,
he catches snow
with his mouth,
framed by concrete, steel, snow –

*no – start again –*

Rewinding
his tongue flicking at the melting flakes
is not the problem
of pain or pleasure I have
with any picture,
the problem is finding something more eloquent
than snow in the mouth,
or a pillar of salt, or a corpse,

because what you always wanted
        was to leave the body,
      what you always wanted
        was to free yourself from pain
        what you always wanted
          was to stop talking
            about it, finally
to free yourself from grievances
        to leave –
The world has a badly designed engine
few would dispute that

it is easier for anyone to say
"My tongue is cold"

than to say
"My heart is broken," that
is the problem –

and for you the world was like
a driverless truck,
you're inside the canopy,
flying towards the ditch
in a slender night –

*no – that's not right –*

the problem is perfect
understanding, how
to tell the story, how to continue
the story in the still night among concrete
and steel, in the wet falling snow
with my son, I keep playing it all
back

## 2   Sound track for 1989

*Q: What newspapers do you read?*
*Thelonious Monk:* "I stopped reading newspapers."

Not after that cold afternoon
in December when Marc Lépine killed fourteen women
unnamed
at the University of Montreal
and then himself

I remember you never liked
my jazz records, it was just
more cultural imperialism to you

*One night Monk danced for a whole set. A lady sitting in the front
called out, "I paid good money to see you." Monk said, "Are you
blind?"*

But you offered violence to yourself
            you fell by your own hand
                you were free
                    of the familiar
                    world
                            you preferred requiems
                            to jazz

(if this is insight
then I'm empty)

Now if the wall falls
in Berlin or a billion children are born, or
you're no longer there –
does anything change?

Would I have let the rain
wash my blood
off a tank in Tiananmen Square?

Would I have walked into a hail of shots
from a semiautomatic in Room 303,
to save anyone
other than myself?

Would I continue
writing this
if I believed
you heard me?

## 3   Leaving the body

I don't know any songs
for this
all I know is
you left early,
you left the imperfect body of the world

and the body is
to be suspected
of beauty
and failure

(whatever the mind grabs and holds
is also suspect)

Don't offer platitudes or simple answers,

do not believe in healing,

do not be angry.

But you suspected everything
when the curtains dropped and you became
a careful
still picture

## 4  Nothing beats silence

Nothing beats silence
when it's a clean
sliver of an arpeggio
you worship
the impossibly beautiful
unplayable note

*Ideal self-aspiration, low self-esteem, high risk potential*
(I give you these labels as additional truths)

Nothing beats silence
except when you're up against
the inarticulate,
an unfinished letter
that keeps turning up
when you clean the basement

## 5   Technology replaces nature as the proper subject of lyric poetry

Risking everything
on your ability to stop
playing since
> tunes are out of date
> the poem is dead
> (elegies presume life
> once was,
> the poem is dead,
> this is an elegy).
> Authors are dead too, of course
there's nothing to be upset about.
What to ask?

Ask why your pain was private,
compressed with a digital algorithm.

Ask why no one played
the saxophone until
the small perfect earth fit
on a diskette, a magnetic trace
of anger, of speech,

*please*
*do not be angry*

(technology replaces nature as
the proper subject of lyric poetry)

you said
*please*
*do not be angry.*

When I know what to say
I'll start shouting.

## 6    Draw me nearer, purple field

Your body wrapped in a too-tight
suit, sharp tang of skunk on the highway
through the air conditioning,
Miles Davis is played in elevators, a fit

If it's a wonderful world
draw me nearer
if it's not
draw me nearer –

nobody notices the shadows
in Wim Wenders movies like you did or
Monk hitting the piano
so hard it goes out of tune, a kind

of new note blowing
away, rolling over Louis Armstrong,
cancelling death, destiny, finding

If it's a wonderful world
draw me nearer
if it's not
draw me nearer –

the big words. No more
swing, no more pain.
Just a syncopated melody
over a regular beat. No more pain

sing the Five Blind Boys,
have you seen this picture of my kid –
draw me nearer
I don't understand what release is –
you leave your body

slowly, drifting
over a field of purple crocuses

# Ending with music

*for Lenny Breau*

He is burning in that furnace of creation.

—Leonard Cohen

Falling on your face to save your hands,
small hands brittle on an icy Winnipeg street, Lenny Breau
never made music for ending.

*Your family was Acadian, so psychically displaced*
*they thought they were cowboys, Lone Pine and Betty Cody,*
*from Auburn, Maine, lost in Winnipeg.*
*You played guitar with a thumb-pick,*
*wore Indian robes, played flamenco*
*segues into "My Funny Valentine".*

In the Edmonton video your hair coils
up like wires on a heroin priest,
long right hand nails finding harmonics nobody
else could touch or name, hands
running down the high E string so
much easier than touching flesh.

Where you were, chewing
like a dark rat on an abandoned angel,
Chet Atkins cries with brain cancer,
a human juke box with nothing left but the record
changer clicking
empty, looking for a tune,
looking for Lenny.

*(I need to get composed. I can't*
*talk about Lenny. He was a genius but*
*that's all. He was like a son.)*

Emily's mother threw you out
when she found dead needles in the garage,

frozen, tied up with E-strings
in winter, in Edmonton.

Drowning in junk a rose
pattern on your jacket the stems
are guitar strings the instrument
smells of pinewood, more alive than the flower.

*(The last time you came home to dry out*
*everybody thought it would be the last time*
*you talked about God.)*

The only time the rose looked
like a rose she took off your
jacket, your shirt, put the guitar
in its case, your fingertips uncalloused
now suddenly on her thigh,
no string for a stem, you feel her
voice more than hear it.

You float in the swimming pool,
still
like the framing shot in a film noir.
You think a line
with a stutter-rest, jump into a 13 chord. You have
an ending with music,
but silent.

# My son learns to ride a bike
*for Betsy*

One night before we watch *The Third Man* I think
about border police, unhappy endings,
a hairdo too perfect to be rumpled by bedclothes,
and how on Friday your mouth tasted
sweet and I think about
fathers and sons and

being hungry for life to
change completely and how white
your throat is, and the strength
of your arms and words, and how surprisingly
everything does change
sometimes

When there are enough chairs,
enough for a world of talking where
everyone sits down to wait or write
and minds are not homeless
some disaster flashes by, cries out
Jesus – all of a sudden

(The way you hold your back
scapula slightly folded and tense
that makes me want to touch you there, slowly)
My son is riding a bike –
Shut up and kiss me, I think you thought –
Jesus – is it his first time?

## Acknowledgements

Some of these poems have appeared, in earlier versions, in the following publications:
*Border Crossings, Grain, The New Quarterly, Prairie Fire,* the anthology *Visions and Realities* (Hyperion Press), the *Mennonite Mirror, Rhubarb,* and online at *Redneck,* <www.wtc.ccinet.ab.ca/tedyck/frames2.htm >.

I am grateful to the Manitoba Arts Council for financial assistance.

Thanks to people who read this manuscript in development, especially Patrick Friesen, and my editor at Brick Books, Barry Dempster. I also want to thank a few early readers of my work: Alida Noble, Esther Wiens, Scott Ellis and Valdine Clemens. Finally, I thank my wife, Elizabeth Troutt, for being practical, lovely, and supportive.

The epigraph and quotations in "Norman Vincent Peale visits Saskatchewan, 1933," are from *Thought Conditioners,* by Norman Vincent Peale, Sermon Publications, 1951. The song lyrics in "Memento, Version 2, Alzheimer's," are from "Deep in a Dream," words by Eddie DeLange, music by Jimmy Van Heusen. The song lyric in "Grandfather, retired, dreams a tell-tale heart," is from "Your Cheatin' Heart," words and music by Hank Williams.

## Biography

Maurice Mierau is a Winnipeg writer who has published
poetry, fiction, and reviews since the mid-1980s. He was born
in the United States and grew up in Africa, the Caribbean, the
U.S., and Saskatchewan, and continues to be fascinated by the
violence and vitality of American culture. His family
background includes Mennonites who are extremely religious
and also those who have made a religion of atheism. Maurice
has a long-standing interest in jazz, and plays the upright bass
with a Winnipeg jazz group. His other obsessions include old
Hollywood movies, science fiction and basketball. Maurice
has spent most of his working life either selling or explaining
computer technology, working in sales and as a technical
writer. He does not believe technology is improving people's
lives. Maurice has a fifteen year old son who is highly
computer literate. His wife Betsy Troutt is an American.
Maurice maintains a website at <www.mauricemierau.com>.